FIRST QUARTER QUARTER SECOND DOWN

DERRICK JOHN WIGGINS

authorHOUSE®

AuthorHouse™
1663 Liberty Drive
Bloomington, IN 47403
www.authorhouse.com
Phone: 1 (800) 839-8640

Published by AuthorHouse 07/01/2020

ISBN: 978-1-7283-6584-8 (sc)
ISBN: 978-1-7283-6585-5 (e)

Nations may rise and fall but an idea lives on.

—John F. Kennedy

FIRESIDE TWEETS

Global Disease Quarantine

Your silence will not protect you. Not every crisis can be managed. We can't protect ourselves from everything. If we want to embrace life, we have to embrace chaos. Life lived in fear is a life half lived. On epidemics, I suggest listening to the clever person in the room or the best lightning rod for your protection, which would be your spine.

—Sarah Hughes

CHAPTER 1

Monday

6:00 a.m.

Jogging, jazz, and building dioramas were meditation to him.

Joseph Bailey had two more blocks to go as his feet pounded the pavement in rhythm. He slightly closed his eyes, sensing his rapid but steady heartbeat. He appreciated the smell of blooming flowers and the sight of cherry blossom trees. He contemplated the ruddy sky. The days were getting longer.

Running was his quiet time. That morning, he reflected not only on his ability to build art but also on his livelihood. His brothers and some of his friends said he was crazy for protecting a president, especially a female one. He personally didn't care whether the president was male or female. A female president was probably better for the country, he thought. The thing was, were Americans ready for a woman president, let alone an African American woman president?

America had never had a female commander in chief. The world, ahead of the United States, already had female leaders, including Martinez of Argentina, Hsian of India, and Arteaga Serrano of Ecuador. Though support for a female head of state had risen in the United States in the last couple of years, still no such president had been elected—until now. It was a historic time in America, with more women than ever running for the presidency. Her time had been destined to happen.

Sarah Jefferson Hughes, he believed, brought the feel of Shirley Chisholm of 1972. At that time, some folks hadn't taken Chisholm seriously. Hughes, on the other hand, was a celebrity to many Americans. *Well, for one thing*, he thought, *whether you like the idea of a woman in power or not, the world has already had many successful female leaders.* Nowadays, polls swung in favor of how much popularity one had rather than his or her skills as a politician.

Five more minutes until he was done. Sweating and panting but controlled, he jogged the last block. He trotted to a gate and swiped his card and then let himself in when the fence opened. Nodding at the watchman in the booth, he removed his Bluetooth headphones, which were now resonating John Coltrane.

"What's your time today?" the watchman asked.

"Forty-five minutes," he answered.

"That was pretty quick. Wish I could do that every day."

"I felt good this morning." He shrugged and walked up a ramp. *Keep it moving*, he thought. The morning air always gave him a chill, particularly after jogging six miles.

He and the security officer exchanged words most dawns after his run, at six o'clock or a quarter to, depending on how he felt.

He swiped his card again and walked into one of the five-story surveillance condominiums in the immaculate neighborhood. He took the elevator to the fourth floor, unlocked his door, flipped his keys onto a desk, and turned on the Bose Wave SoundTouch radio. He didn't have to turn to a station; his connected Bluetooth continued the melodies.

He owned an average-size one-bedroom bachelor pad, not too dirty and not too clean. Replica kit ships, destroyers, and war planes big and small, old and new, were encased in glass shrines around his apartment, in neat corners.

As he took a shower, he contemplated his daily duties. He had to be at work by seven o'clock sharp and had to be observant for almost ten hours—or sometimes, out of the blue, sixteen. That day, if everything went on schedule, he'd be out of there in under ten. The president was a prompt individual. That day, Bailey and his team were reserved for a bunch of meetings, and then he would return home to model building and the soothing sounds of ragtime.

Four months before the general election until now, Joseph Bailey had protected and gotten to know Madam Hughes. They had now gotten through the first hundred days of the administration. He called the first hundred days "the first down," and the Hughes administration had gained much ground. Now they were in the second.

Bailey approached work the way he did his hobby: with patience and a flawless attention to detail. He was a perfectionist, and Hughes knew it. He had personally picked his team, who were impeccable. Within the first month of Hughes's presidency, Bailey's team had been given the title special agent detail to the president, or SADP. Around the White House, they called his team the Gestapo.

His other relationship with the president was weirdly flirtatious. She would blatantly, facetiously try to court him. He would lightheartedly decline. Though neither of them were dating, he thought it peculiar and too controversial to date the most influential and richest woman in the world. Maybe after four or eight years, he'd accept her propositions. He chuckled to himself. He'd be an old man by then.

President Hughes was an exquisite, athletic thirty-six-year-old woman. If Bailey allowed his animal instincts to take over, he surely would succumb to her advances and have to relinquish his career. But he treasured his profession, and being the gentleman he was, he held back.

Hughes was a workhorse—some would have said an anomaly. He knew that by now, she had probably just finished her morning run on the treadmill and was doing a core workout while watching CNN, reading the *Huffington Post* online, and talking to Clark, her director of national intelligence. She multitasked well enough to chat with Clark about the President's Daily Brief and know what she read and saw. He had seen her do it, and sometimes she even had McCarthy, her senior chief of staff, there too. She reminded him of the Bionic Woman, running on an exercise machine while scientists observed and gossiped, and of the multitasking of his own mother.

Hughes had started life young. She'd served in the military at eighteen years old while attending night classes at Harvard until she turned twenty-two. She had owned a million-dollar software company at twenty-three and become the first female mayor of New York City at twenty-five. She had been the first Independent to be supported by think tanks, super PACs, lobbyists, progressives, libertarians, and celebrities alike. She was a prodigy in her own right, a regular GI Jane. He often had wondered during her presidential campaign whether she really needed to caucus with the Democrats.

The mass media characterized her as well read, sarcastic in a humorous way, and a bit condescending to outside circles. Her mid-Atlantic manner was famously distinguished. Her race connected her to minorities, and her transatlantic accent appealed to the majority of Americans. To her assistants, she was complex. They described her as observant and witty—a global cosmopolitan.

After showering and dressing in his black uniform, Bailey reckoned spraying himself with a little Creed Aventus wouldn't hurt anybody. From his residence in Adams Morgan, it would take him ten minutes to drive into Washington, DC, into another day at the office.

His life right now was about the president's journey. Journalists had whispered that it might be possible for a third party to bring Democrats and Republicans together. Madam Hughes had given the United States its first female president. She moved about her profession with simplicity.

Gone for now was the early campaign rhetoric that a child would be running the nation with a bunch of nerds and misplaced sincerity. Many Americans had already forgotten the town hall healing conventions Hughes had hosted during her presidential campaign. Americans had not forgotten that she was by far the youngest president in history; for that, she had been nicknamed the Little Lioness. Bailey wanted to be part of that history, and he was smack dab in the middle of it. He smiled. He loved being apolitical, loved his country, and most of all, loved God.

FIRESIDE TWEETS

Israeli-Palestinian Conflict

Palestinian, Hamas, and Israeli leaders have to agree that the West Bank, like the Gaza Strip, should be governed by Hamas and the PLO. If Israeli settlers settle in the West Bank because it's cheap, they should be governed by the PLO. In reality, they are not. In the States, this reality is called a form of gentrification by Israel.

—Sarah Hughes

CHAPTER 2

7:00 a.m.

The president was meticulous, if anything, so Bailey knew she was getting dressed in front of him on purpose. As he watched her fasten her cyan shirt, he peeked at her smooth desert-sand belly. He'd meant to glance at her petite cleavage, but it was already hidden in a tight bra. Trying to ease— or, better yet, erase—his chauvinism, he wondered why the president had called him into her private quarters again.

This was the third morning she had invited him into the master bedroom of the White House. The first time had been to discuss the black budget and covert operations; the second had been to create the SADP. He had no clue what they would be discussing that day, but he knew it had to be something clandestine.

The bedroom had a traditional look; to him, it resembled an expensive hotel lodging, with an auburn canopy bed. Vanilla-fragranced reed diffusers dotted Hughes's living quarters and her office in the West Wing. Her usual sunrise glass of white zin sat on the bureau, next to an autographed photo of Bruce Lee and a monitor projecting Fox live.

She wiped lint off a sapphire suit jacket hanging on the back of an armchair.

"Madam, we have people for that," Bailey said, grinning.

Hughes ignored him. "GIs are appearing more like dreamboats every day," she mumbled.

Bailey raised an eyebrow as if to say, "Excuse me?" *Here she goes again with her peculiar intentions, early in the morning.*

She then spoke clearly and almost pleadingly. "I was wondering if you could draw me a lofty contract."

"Sure, Madam, what's up? Better yet, as you would say, what's cooking?"

She moved to her classical-style cheval glass and poked at her short, curly russet hair. "I'm having dinner with Ivankov on Friday. Was wondering if you would accompany me."

She turned to face him, and he detected her searching his facial expression for an answer.

"Of course, yes, ma'am. I and—"

"No, not as a GI. I want you to *accompany me* in a dinner suit and tie. I know it's short notice. It's just to set an image—nothing attached."

"Is this for undercover purposes?"

She waved off his question. "Holy Joe! Can you do it?"

He spoke nervously, not knowing what the president's intentions were. She could be flirtatious at times and dead serious the next minute. "Well, this could open a can of worms. People might, well, think it's permanent. We might have to continue this propaganda. For how long?"

"It'll end the same night. I'll make a statement. You'll be like a chaperone."

With uncertainty still in his voice, he asked, "Your personal protection—your escort?"

"You don't have to decide now. Give me an answer by tomorrow night." She took a sip of her wine.

There was a knock at the door.

"Come in," Hughes said.

Bailey knew his private morning with the president was over. He nodded before moving toward the door. "Ma'am."

She smirked. "Stick around. We have official biz, you know."

He raised his eyebrow again. It was obvious she had more to say. Usually, meetings like that took place in the Oval Office.

McCarthy walked in with a small notepad in hand.

Hughes spoke while eyeing the news. "Kev, what are the senators and representatives buzzing about pertaining to academic reform and health care?"

Kevin McCarthy glanced at Bailey but spoke as if he weren't there. Bailey wondered if McCarthy was jealous—not envious in a sexual way but relationship-wise.

Senior Chief of Staff Kevin McCarthy, whose portfolio included work in public policy and intergovernmental affairs, had grown with the president through college, the Marine Corps, and campaigns. Bailey, on the other hand, had been acquainted with Hughes for only about eight months, so McCarthy's slight protectiveness was duly noted. They both were handsome men, though Bailey felt his minor edge was that he wasn't married with kids.

"They're still debating your single-payer executive," McCarthy replied. "The debate this time isn't on the cost of your Medicaid-care but on lowering the cost of drugs, which they're saying is affecting private companies."

Hughes slipped on her jacket and changed the channel to MSNBC. "Showing them that this fit into the budget meant nothing. Still, there's beef. I'm sure Congress is still working on ways to stop our student work program."

McCarthy smiled. "Yes, they say the older veterans aren't pulling their weight of fifteen hours a week."

Bailey laughed to himself as he watched the president shake her head in displeasure. During Hughes's first week in office, she'd signed an executive order mandating that all families who were unemployed or made less than $125,000 would have free tuition at all state universities. To retain those benefits, one had to maintain a 2.7 GPA and, if unemployed, work in the fifteen-hour program. The order also included free state college for veterans, no matter their income, as long as they met the GPA requirement and were part of the student work program.

In Bailey's heart, he felt that her attempt to universalize free health care and college was noble. He, for one, didn't care about such things. His family never had known the woes of paying for college or health care. His father had been in the United States Air Force, and his mother had been a prosecutor. They had paid for his schooling, so his education had been free. His two younger brothers also hadn't had to face the anguish of currency.

His career interest was principally analyzing federal and national enforcement security. His squad had a strong belief that there could be no privacy if you wanted security.

Hughes, holding her wineglass, stood in front of the screen, sipping. A female news anchor explained the day's predictions for the Dow Jones Industrial Average and the Nasdaq Stock Market.

"Where are we with mortgage tax breaks?" Hughes asked. "I knew deducting 50 percent from homeowners' federal taxes would warrant many rhubarbs from Congress."

"Yes, that'll be your six o'clock," McCarthy said. He looked down at his pad. "Mortgage tax breaks for solar panels and wind turbines."

"Joe will be on tight detail when we greet the Russian president," Hughes said. "What do you think of him accompanying me to this banquet?"

"Morning," McCarthy said, finally acknowledging Bailey in the room.

Bailey nodded and said good morning under his breath.

"Audacious move," McCarthy said in answer to Hughes's query. "I think the media are going to be all over it and say you two are a couple. On the other hand, the Russian president is bringing his wife."

"So your thoughts?" Hughes asked again.

"I personally don't agree with it," McCarthy said, glancing at Bailey. "Although"—he shrugged—"maybe the country is ready to see you in a relationship. You're damned if you do or don't. Remember they came after you for not being married, saying they haven't seen anything like this since Buchanan. Who better to date but your personal SS agent?"

Bailey recognized McCarthy's last statement as sarcasm and noticed Hughes did too.

"Not date. Fire extinguisher," Hughes said.

"The world will see it as a date."

"Well, he has until tomorrow night to decide."

"So you've already decided," McCarthy said. He glanced at Hughes and then looked directly at Bailey and leered. "It's all up to you now."

"With Ivankov there, flapping lips won't be focused on who I'm dating," Hughes said, "but on supporting North Korean immigrants who are pouring a lot of moolah directly back into the DPRK regime, deflecting our sanctions."

"Mr. Bailey will have to be briefed," McCarthy said. "If he decides to go, that is."

Bailey folded his arms and gave his own smug look.

Hughes sank into a chair, careful not to spill her drink. "It's back to you, Joe. What bad biz awaits me for the day?"

He had to admit the president had surprised him that morning with the dinner invite, but he was not flabbergasted on detail when it came to perils. Hostility was his specialty.

Bailey cleared his throat. "Madam, threats from the ANU have been quiet, though yesterday we arrested a suspected affiliate. We're not sure yet on his intentions; we're interrogating him as we speak."

He watched Hughes cross her legs. She was concerned.

"What do we have?" she asked.

"John Herman, a clothing designer, had been following you for days.

Wrote a bunch of things on Facebook about how the government owed him money. He's against your new taxes on the wealthy."

"Hope we have probable cause and are not just sending citizens to crowbar hotels for the sake of fear."

Bailey smiled. "Sorry, Madam, but the NDAA bill says we could. We also traced some of his offshore accounts funding Duran."

"Interesting," Hughes said. "That explains his intentions."

She gazed at Bailey as he spoke about the detaining. He couldn't tell if it was a carnal or somber look.

Arthur Duran—probably not his or her real name—was an anarchist, Tea Party sympathizer, and secessionist. He or she was the leader of a home-grown terrorist group called Activists for Nationalist United, the ANU. Affiliates of the group were unknown; theoretically, there were about 150 members. The USSS and the FBI already had arrested ten members in under a year.

Worst of all, Duran was a black-hat spyware hacker. Duran's main intent was to steal money from banks to fund conservative right-wing parties throughout the country. The ANU was the Tea Party's superhero, their Robin Hood, their Zorro. Symbolically, Duran would taunt the authorities with the Gadsden and Betsy Ross flag with a Roman numeral II. "*Sic semper tyrannis*" was the signature Duran used after writing threatening emails to the president. Throughout the course of her presidential career, individuals had called her a feminazi, a baby killer, and a racist nigger bitch. One person had written, "I want to rape and kill you, you sacrilegious whore. I want you decapitated," and had painted her face on pornographic material. The perpetrators were not arrested right away but were tracked. The SADP knew exactly who they were. Some were wealthy, some were poverty-stricken, and some had regular nine-to-five jobs.

Sic semper tyrannis, the words the ANU threatened with, translated from Latin, meant "Thus always to tyrants." That was what John Wilkes Booth had shouted after shooting Abraham Lincoln.

The USSS, FBI, and SADP had made Arthur Duran and the ANU *hostis publicus*—"public enemy"—number one.

FIRESIDE TWEETS

Brexit

The question is are referendums good for democracy? Should the majority rule and give the country back to its people? Is it tyranny of the majority, or should there be constitutional amendments? Like voting for elected officials in a representative democracy. Well, Brexit means Brexit. I can't speak for the British, but I hope they stay with the EU. If you want to go fast, go alone. If you want to go far, go together. None of us is as smart as all of us.

—Sarah Hughes

CHAPTER 3

8:00 a.m.

Immigration was another issue Bailey had no interest in. For at least three generations, his family had been born in the United States. On his father's side, he had some Blackfoot in his DNA, which he believed made him more American than the average American of European descent. However, Bailey recognized he had to sit back and listen to the white noise and confusion of the countries' debates on the topic.

Immigration mattered to a lot of people, and that issue was one of the reasons threats to the president soared. Eighty-five guests populated the State Floor, in the largest room of the mansion. He'd screened them all for a week and knew a paper trail of their lives. He knew most were Mexican, along with a trickle of Chinese and South Asian Indians and one Ethiopian fellow. Some were still in legal battles over being extradited, but most were legal immigrants with problems of family members being deported. Bailey and eight field agents were in the room. The agents, in plain clothes, were sitting among the group. Bailey smiled to himself. *Let's get this town hall meeting underway.* The attendees had forty minutes.

Sitting in between the large portraits of Martha and George Washington, Hughes crossed her legs, and the meeting began. Olivia Allen, a reporter from CNN, sitting adjacent to the president, hosted the East Room town hall meeting. Allen introduced herself and the president to the cameras and the group, who sat on slightly elevated padded bleachers facing them.

Hughes introduced herself with her renowned "Howdy, everybody." She then explained her Immigration System Program, executive order 14165. The media called it her ISP initiative. It had gained positive and negative responses in the press and from many Americans across the country. Now she got to clarify her initiative during the town hall, which was going to air that night.

Hughes explained that she supported the Dream Act and DACA, and her order would not eradicate those programs. Her agenda was focused on making America's twelve million illegal immigrants legal within a month if they filled out the ISP application. The requirements that had to be met were no criminal record and full disclosure of one's livelihood. The admission was at an inexpensive price of $300.

She then described why the order was not yet implemented. Many midwestern and southern senators had sued her administration. Though the bill had passed Congress—barely—one Supreme Court judge had blocked it. She now had to take her project to the Fifth Circuit Court of Appeals. The president assured the group before her that the Fourteenth Amendment would inevitably persuade the courts.

One thing Bailey knew about President Hughes was that she was a magnificent debater and skilled orator. She was impressive at conveying stories and information and explaining why the bill had made it that far. She answered a few questions out of many from the bunch. The first inquiry came from someone who had been born in the United States and worked for NASA. He told the president he was working hard at keeping his mother, who was an illegal immigrant, in the country. He wanted to know how the ISP order was going to help his mom.

"The Immigration System Program," Hughes said, "will naturalize your mother within a month. There's a three-hundred-greenback application fee, and she'll have to fill out the application online. The fee will also include the biometrics cost. This system will quickly do away with the green card as we know it and make your mom a permanent citizen for life with no renewals."

Another question was from a lady who was a citizen and whose husband had been deported by ICE. She said she'd heard of many other similar stories. She asked, "When will this order go through, and what can be done now?"

"I will personally have some people look into your situation and work out the details in finding out if ICE did this legally or illegally. That's why it's imperative this order goes through. That's why it's crucial for you, as a citizen, to vote. You're not just voting for yourselves but for your families."

The final question was from a college student. He felt Republicans and Democrats in Congress always went back and forth with the same issues and never got anything done. Why was her order any different?

"Remember: I'm an Independent, so—"

The assembly laughed.

"So I feel your frustration on the matter. Bureaucracy in this country is a megillah or, better yet, a slow-moving ocean liner. To speed up these proceedings, you'll need a politician who's concerned about issues rather than the basis of a political ideology or partisanship."

Bailey remembered her saying at her State of Union address, "No human is stronger than the momentum of history." The nation was truly evolving, because so far, they hadn't stopped this Independent female African American politician, and America hadn't seen an Independent president since George Washington.

However, he knew there was a darker side to her that wasn't so publicized. Many people across the country feared ISP. President Hughes didn't gossip much in the media about those qualms; rather, she answered them through action. She had tightened border security and conducted thorough investigations on twelve million illegal immigrants. She would briefly speak on that, but her words were only partially true. She didn't lie; she just didn't tell the whole truth.

Bailey knew that long before ISP had been drafted, Hughes had closed down many military bases in Africa, Japan, and Germany and on an island in the Indian Ocean called Diego Garcia. Then she'd structured fifteen additional US military bases along the Mexican border, mostly in Texas and Arizona. Many unmanned aerial vehicles, or UAVs, were like constant night-and-day eyes buzzing up and down the two-thousand-mile international border. Military UAVs searched for illegal border crossers from above, while a hundred thousand ultrasonic motion detectors listened for man-made burrows below.

The online ISP application was designed to monitor the twelve million illegal immigrants the way law enforcement agencies analyzed criminals. The Hughes administration had already started monitoring thirty million legal immigrants in the States with an NSA method called Project Trailblazer. Thousands of immigrants affiliated with gangs had already been deported by ICE under her presidency.

Reporters had asked Hughes, while she was boarding Marine One, "Why is there military buildup at the southern border?"

She'd responded, spreading her hands out, "We all have to come into this country the correct, smart way."

Immigration was a subject Bailey was not interested in, though he felt Hughes handled it as she handled most things. She often quoted the twenty-sixth president of the United States: "Speak softly, but carry a big stick."

FIRESIDE TWEETS

Ten Terrorists Released Early from Prison in the UK

I will never agree to the premature release of any terrorist, foreign or domestic. We are moving into a world where spy devices are built into every object we encounter. There's not a single app that's not watching you right now.

—Sarah Hughes

CHAPTER 4

9:30 a.m.

Bailey remembered what the Oval Office had looked like under the former president. Now it was swathed in cream-colored wallpaper and a taupe rug with three quotes on the border that he felt represented her style and suited her. One of the quotes was from Hemingway: "Courage is grace under pressure." The second was from Darwin: "It is not the strongest of the species that survive, nor the most intelligent, but the one most responsive to change." The final was a Bible verse: "Good will come to those who are generous and lend freely, who conduct their affairs with justice" (Psalm 112:5).

Besides battleship paintings around the office, there was a portrait of FDR. He remembered Hughes telling him that she felt like Roosevelt: she was handicapped, and she had to hide it, just as he had.

Then there was a model Zumwalt battleship he'd built, which she'd placed on a desk against the wall in the office. He, for some peculiar reason, always looked at it every time he entered the room.

Bailey, standing in the secretary workplace, already knew Vice President Adams, DNI Clark, and Chief of Staff McCarthy were there. They sat around the president on tan sofas in the middle of the room. A body man, Douglas Wise, ushered him into the Oval Office.

"So next Monday we go to Oregon to promote the AFP order. I have it straight," Hughes said.

She gestured for Bailey to sit anywhere on the couch.

He glanced at his model boat and sat next to Clark, diagonally from Hughes. They all had open laptops, coffee, tea, and Danish pastries on a brown table in front of them.

Hughes had finished talking about Oregon, and Bailey knew he had to prepare for the huge excursion to Shepherds Flat Wind Farm. Congress barely had approved her executive order 14166, the Alternative Fuel Program, or AFP. She continued promoting the program to ensure its integrity.

In her semiboring speeches across the country, she explained that in fifty years, the world would consume all of its oil. The United States, the largest consumer of oil, consumed 20 percent of the world's oil per day. Her program pushed many companies in the direction of wind, solar, and hydroelectric power. Companies and cities who used those energies were now exempt from federal taxes. Anyone who owned and drove an electric car also was exempt from federal taxes.

The law also included a three-year clause. All bus companies in every state had to run their buses on electric power. All gas stations had to have hybrid-vehicle chargers. The bus companies and gas stations had three years to comply, after which they had to pay heavy fines.

That, of course, caused a global economic impact on the oil industry and OPEC and seemed to displease the minister of petroleum and natural resources in Saudi Arabia. Bailey figured that was what they'd been talking about before he entered the office.

Hughes put on what she liked to call her reading cheaters, set her laptop next to her, and typed on the computer. "One more thing before we get started. Let's have the governors' meeting moved to Wednesday. I'll tell Velerie."

Bailey also knew about the governors' meeting she'd just moved back to Wednesday. The governors from Texas, Florida, New Jersey, and West Virginia would be meeting in the White House about the capital punishment directive. Executive order 14167 sanctioned all states to have the death penalty. As controversial as the subject was, it was no surprise to him that Congress had overturned it, saying it was unconstitutional. He knew she was going to veto the decision but wanted to discuss the situation with governors on both sides of the argument. She had done the same when she was mayor, and for the first time since 1995, she'd reinstated the death penalty in New York City.

Hughes looked directly at Bailey. "I need you to collaborate with Clark on the latest ANU threats. They may be funding Al-Qaeda in the Arabian Peninsula. Probably instigating larger attacks. We believe ANU is reaching out to outside terrorists to prove this administration is a dud. If we are attacked, the media and politicians will say it's because I closed too many military bases around the world."

"We're going to need bank-account-hacking signature transactions." Clark spoke quickly and precisely. "We've now labeled Duran as an elite cyberterrorist hacker. Interpol has already been alerted."

"We've two years' worth of data on ANU and Duran," Bailey said. "I have to admit the ANU have increased their threats since this administration has taken office. We've also worked closely with the FBI on this. We're going to have to set up a day to compare notes."

Clark looked down at his computer, finding his calendar schedule. "Can we set up a meeting tomorrow, like noon, with you and the FBI lead on this case?"

"Sure, I'll set it up for tomorrow." Bailey scrutinized everyone in the Oval Office before he saw himself out.

McCarthy was his usual grumpy self, and VP Nelson Adams was chatty and watchful, his predictable self. Bailey saw them all as tenured white men who had been in politics too long.

Then there was DNI Peter Clark, the oldest of the group. Bailey didn't know much about him, except he had been an FBI field agent, director of the CIA, and secretary of Homeland Security. Bailey never could read him but knew he was a statistics-collecting fanatic.

President Hughes did not once look at Bailey as she did in her private quarters. She wore her no-nonsense game face in front of these weathered men. "Send in the lieutenant general and his commanders on your way out," she told Bailey without looking up from her laptop.

Bailey ushered in the lieutenant general and five of his chief officers of the United States Army Corps of Engineers. He realized the president was now about to get into a deep debate with that federal agency about restoring wetlands around the country, starting with New Orleans. She had been disputing with the agency since she'd gained office. She did not look ecstatic as he closed the door behind him.

He focused on and worried about his own appointment, preparing himself in his head. Bailey knew Senior Special Agent Chuck Hellbender enough to know that tomorrow's noon meeting was going to have one voice. Hellbender was an eccentric anomaly to the human race. He also had been diagnosed with autism and had an aptitude for solving mysteries and puzzles. He had been in the FBI for four years and single-handedly had solved more than a hundred bank robberies and investigations into organized and terrorist crime.

The FBI had nicknamed him Agent Foreshadow. The name was fitting for Hellbender because when he took cases, it seemed as if he already knew the criminals' motives. Hellbender loved his nickname and also dubbed himself Foreshadow on a game called *After Pulse* that he relentlessly played online. Bailey knew Hellbender was a virtuoso at the game, which gave him confidence to be like a superhero in the real world.

Though Hellbender was probably the best weapon the FBI ever had had, his only relationship to the outside world was through online games. His only lingo was the internet. Bailey knew he himself was going to be the one voice at the meeting.

FIRESIDE TWEETS

Israeli Forces Kill Seventeen-Year-Old Demonstrator in the West Bank

I believe in the freeze of settlements. They are not necessary for the security of Israel. We must have negotiations for PLO rule in the region. The cause of violence is not ignorance but self-interest. Only reverence can restrain violence: reverence for human life and its environment.

—Sarah Hughes

CHAPTER 5

Iceland

2:30 p.m.

Ian Blair really wanted to play golf that day and not attend the rendezvous. Every time he visited Reykjavik, he wanted to play that game and not think about the world. The endless snowcapped mountains in the city were beautiful, he thought. *Keep thinking about the mountains*, he told himself. Blair looked at his watch as his friend sat down before him in the Austurvöllur Café.

Blair sipped his tea. "You're late."

Robertson waved for a waitress. "My security detail suggested I take an alternate route today."

Blair gave a smirk of disbelief. He had security too, and they never made him late. *You have to plan for these things, man.*

"I'm more renowned than you," Robertson said. "I have more channels to go through."

Ian Blair knew Joel Robertson was telling the truth. Robertson was an American televangelist and secretly the leader of the charismatic movement. Blair knew that as an economist who controlled a Fortune 500 pharmaceutical company, he was billions of dollars richer than his old friend. He'd rather be rich than famous. "We're playing the popularity game now?"

When the waitress came, Robertson ordered a coffee, black and sweet. "We're going to have to set up a second meeting, you know," Robertson said.

"I know," Blair responded. "I wanted to talk to you privately before we spread the news."

Though the small restaurant wasn't too crowded, Blair had had his protection sit at tables around him and his companion. Besides his men, they would be out of earshot of whoever came into the bistro.

When the young waitress came back with the coffee, they ordered food. Robertson requested fish stew, and Blair ordered the lamb soup with rye bread. "Hughes has closed bases in Kosovo and Germany and totally pulled out of Afghanistan," Blair said.

"I haven't heard about the Afghani bases."

"That's because it hasn't come out yet." Blair sipped his tea again. "Hughes is going to give a speech about it tomorrow at a press briefing."

"What the fuck is POTUS doing, Ian? She'll upset assured interest in those regions."

"We have bigger problems."

"Can't envision anything bigger than this."

"She can pretty much do what she wants with the military. As much as you may hate to hear this, she is commander in chief."

"As if crippling the industrial complex isn't enough."

Blair spoke softly. "Remember when we said she was the most inquisitive, naive fox we ever knew?"

"Yeah, her first day in office—asking for the Kennedy files and Project Blue Book." Robertson shook his head, disgusted. "Who does that? There are much more important things leaders of the free world need to do."

"You already know she's micromanaging the CIA and NSA and has now stumbled upon Project Safeguard."

"Safeguard—that's part of the MDA?"

"You're not that old."

"We already anticipated this." Robertson shrugged.

"Chances of her knowing about the ESM project are now heightened."

Robertson's eyes widened in bewilderment as the waitress served their food. He waited for the attendant to leave before he spoke. "Wasn't disclosing Safeguard enough? She preaches transparency. How long before our enemies will know?"

"You mean China?"

"I mean anybody."

"For about a month, only she and top US military officials knew about it." Blair watched Robertson breathe a little. *At least the president can keep a secret—for now. If the world knew Project Safeguard worked, there would be foreign spies all over America, especially from China and Russia.*

They had created an accurate long-range plasma-burst arsenal that could take out ballistic missiles from all countries. The military had already equipped it in ten satellites and almost every base around the world. In 1983, they'd called it SDI, nicknamed Star Wars, under Ronald Regan. Blair had to smile to himself. Yes, almost thirty-five years later, they'd gotten it to work.

Unless the world was in peril, they vowed never to tell anyone, least of all the president of the United States. They definitely weren't going to tell Hughes. She was exceedingly meddlesome, though. Hughes had investigated the project and found its core deep in the Ozark Mountains. *Big problem,* Blair thought, *because Project ESM was developed in the same place.*

"Damn that fox. We're going to have to relocate the ESM project," Robertson said with disappointment.

Blair sipped his soup from his spoon and nodded in agreement. "I say as long as she's in power, keep America's foreign trade complicated. We make it unbearable, a thorn in her side, to keep her mind off our secrets."

"Done. Agreed," Robertson said.

As he watched Robertson consume his food, Blair smiled to himself again comfortably—for now. All Blair could think about at the moment were those beautiful snow-crested mountains and a game of golf.

FIRESIDE TWEETS

Turkey–United States Relations

Considering the PKK terrorist group; Syrian refugees; the MIT scandal of supplying weapons to Syria; the 2016 coup d'état attempt; and the United States not giving up Fethullah Gülen and Reza Zarrab, an Iranian-born, Turkey-based businessman evading US sanctions on Iran, Turkey is supposed to be our ally. Scars fade with time, but the ones that fester build character and caution.

—Sarah Hughes

CHAPTER 6

Tuesday

12:00 p.m.

They all sat at the end of a large conference table next to a fireplace with the portrait portraying Teddy Roosevelt as a Rough Rider hanging over its mantel.

"I'm sending you the information on the individuals we confined," the deputy director of the FBI, Andrew Giuliani, said. He stared across the table at Clark, making sure he received the secure email message sent to the DNI's protected laptop.

"Got it," Clark responded.

"I'm also sending figures of a warehouse raid we did in Wichita," Bailey said, and he clicked Send on his protected laptop inbox. Seated adjacent to Clark, he waited until Clark nodded, confirming he'd gotten the email. "We also have pseudonyms Duran uses and letters Duran sent to the president. I made duplicates of the letters." He took out some papers from his manila folder and handed them to Clark.

Clark scrutinized the documents for a moment and then put the papers in his own folder, which read "Classified." "Can you guys brief me on who we incarcerated and the pseudonyms?"

Bailey put his hand out for Giuliani to go first. As Giuliani spoke about the ten detained ANU members, Bailey glanced at Hellbender, who sat athwart from him.

Hellbender had an open *PC Gamer* magazine next to his confidential notes. Bailey watched him flip through the periodical while still jotting down details about their conference. He knew Hellbender was special like that.

"This recent guy we apprehended," Giuliani said, "owns a small-time clothing company. Besides Mr. Herman stalking the president, these ANU constituents have signature MOs. They're different-level hackers. We're characterizing them as militarist and dominionist. They're emerging rightist, new-age dominion theologists."

Clark nodded at Bailey to begin his synopsis.

"Our white hats have learned who was attacking banks across the States with viruses," Bailey said. "Duran used prominent names from Zionist and Christian right preachers, using diminutives like Hunt, Falwell, and Lindsey as to who owned the IP addresses. IP number tracking soon led us to a secluded warehouse in Kansas. We didn't find any assailant or assailants. We did find remnants of a massive database system set up."

"So you just missed them?" Clark asked.

Bailey nodded. "We found passageways built under the warehouse leading into the flatlands near Garden Plain. Where the tunnels ended in the flats, tire tracks were revealed. After analyzing the tire impressions, we know the individual or individuals drove away in trailers."

The door opened, and Hughes walked into the Roosevelt Room. "Howdy."

Everyone stood, except Hellbender, who kept reading his magazine. Hughes, wearing square reading glasses, put her hand up for everyone to sit. As they sat, Bailey saw that the left side of her face was swollen, and her bottom lip was cut.

Her fresh scars reminded him that she'd had Brazilian jujitsu lessons that morning. Bailey never understood why she physically went so hard on her sparring partners. He guessed she was condescending in her matches, shouting statements like "You're a bunch of flat tires—roll up your flaps, you sad Sam, and hit me!" so they would hit her harder. *Her competitive trash-talking got her those lumps. She was basically busting their chops.* He presumed she'd learned her toughness from her parents, her four years in the USMC, or both.

Her eyeglasses, her makeup, and her beauty had hidden her contusions well at the 9:00 a.m. briefing. The bruises hadn't shown much when he watched her on TV as she answered questions in the Press Briefing Room about her slow extraction from Afghanistan and Iraq. She'd preached to the American press and world that all bases would be closed in Afghanistan and Iraq except for bases in Kabul and Baghdad. She'd promised the endeavor would be completed in eight months and suggested other countries with forces in the region do likewise. Some funds and security training still would be given to the Afghani and Iraqi governments.

As she sat next to Bailey, she grinned. "Please continue."

"Madam President," Bailey said, acknowledging Hughes. He then looked at Clark. "We identified that the tires fit a Honda Ram towing a gooseneck camper trailer. We also know the perp wore Timberland boots, from prints in the soil."

After Bailey nodded to indicate he was finished, Clark surveyed his laptop for a minute. "What I'm about to utter is highly sensitive material. We're positive this Duran is the same black hat who is not only funding and giving away money at rallies around the country but also funding terrorists in Yemen and Somalia.

"We also believe Duran cyberattacked all twelve branches of the Federal Reserve and stole eighty million dollars. This isn't only an act of terrorism but an act of espionage and treason."

"A great number of Americans are still displeased about my agnosticism," Hughes said. "An attack on the Fed is a direct attack on me. These so-called new-age dominionists will stop at nothing to see my downfall. I thought these conservative Christian Zionists believed Jesus is all about love."

"Can I have a copy of those letters to the president?" Hellbender asked.

"Sure," Bailey responded. He handed his extra copies of Duran's letters to Hellbender. Bailey watched him sift through the five documents. "I'm going to send you all the emails too."

As she looked at Bailey, Hughes's chubby cheeks broadened. She patted him on the thigh and whispered in his ear, "Watch this." With her full attention now on Hellbender, she asked, "Chuck, sir, who do you believe is this cyberattacker Duran and the ANU?"

Giuliani gave Hughes a gaze of annoyance. She glared back deliberately with a blank expression. Bailey laughed to himself at the two individuals. Giuliani felt that when Hellbender communicated, he was always too forthcoming, too bluntly innocent. Bailey knew Hughes loved it.

Hellbender cleared his throat. "Duran is one man who has many followers. He has important financial interest backing him, and they all have deep hatred for you, Madam President. The reason Duran will always be elusive is because there is a leak in the White House. Someone isn't who they seem. But they'll learn the president isn't one to bend to how America has been run for hundreds of years, and they'll seek to kill you." Hellbender glanced at Hughes and then looked down at his open game magazine.

"No shit," Giuliani said, speaking under his breath but loudly enough for everyone to hear.

"So what are we going to do about this?" Hughes asked Hellbender.

"I'm working on it, ma'am," Hellbender responded. He didn't look up from his magazine. "Nothing is going to happen to you, ma'am; we'll solve this. I'm working on this. We'll solve this."

"Thank you, Chuck, for that," Hughes said sincerely.

Until that day, Bailey hadn't known that Duran was messing around with the Federal Reserve. Absorbing up-to-date evidence on his laptop, he noticed how tight-lipped the situation was. Though the Fed had been hacked about fifty times, that information was never told to the public. Seven people, all arrested in the last ten years, had succeeded in stealing thousands of dollars. Duran was the eighth to break through the Fed's cybersecurity and the first to steal millions and get away with it.

They hadn't yet found an infiltrator in the government on the case or if Duran had aloof superiors. Only time would tell if Hellbender was truly as precise a crime solver as they said. He knew for sure Giuliani didn't care for Hellbender, possibly because Giuliani knew that this special-needs person was better than he was. Bailey giggled at that notion of envy and knew Hughes did too.

It was remarkable Hughes could give an essential oration about withdrawing soldiers halfway around the world and then crash that meeting. It was as if she didn't trust her security to protect her and had to make sure the job was done right, micromanaging. Or she was just nosy like that. Knowing her, it was both, and she wasn't finished.

As the meeting ended, everyone shook hands and the gentlemen gathered their belongings. Hughes whispered more in Bailey's ear. "You know how Washington works: quid pro quo. I helped you solve this case. Before you leave work, you have to give me an answer about dinner Friday."

Bailey smirked. She was being her facetious self again, knowing she hadn't solved anything. She gave him a gaze of solemnity that melted through him. For that instant, her dark umber eyes seemed alluring, and he was not a fan of typical brown eyes. He resisted his compulsion to make her wait until the end of the day. She was president of the United States, debatably the most authoritative person in the world.

"I'll see you Friday, Madam President," Bailey muttered.

FIRESIDE TWEETS

Venezuela–United States Relations

Assumptions are the termites of relationships. The United States believes Venezuela transports illegal drugs, supports the Revolutionary Armed Forces of Colombia and has ties with Iran. Venezuela believes the Unites States attempted to destabilize their government by disrupting their military. Venezuela also claims the United States gave their high officials, including Hugo Chávez, cancer. A bad relationship is like standing barefoot on broken glass: if you walk away, you will hurt, but eventually, you will heal.

—Sarah Hughes

CHAPTER 7

Iceland

5:00 p.m.

Blair liked the view of Mount Akrafjall from the water in Faxa Bay. He adored the different zones of weathered rock. Thawing snowcaps created rivulets of ice around stone and foliage to flow out onto beaches before draining into the bay. Mint cream, lime, and tan colors from top to bottom illuminated the mountain, mixed with a haze of ghost-white clouds and azure sky.

Blair had invited his teenage grandkids and cousins of his associates aboard the *Weishaupt*. The *Weishaupt*, his gigayacht of eight decks, was anchored four miles off the coast of Reykjavik. While their families and crew roamed about the ship, he and his colleagues discussed particulars at this second conference. The soundproof spherical room, which was five decks above the sea and had a 360-degree view of the outside, was perfect for another secret assembly, Blair thought.

Another old companion attended this assembly, for a total of three. She'd demanded they have an appetizer before dinner with the rest of the family. Ronda Cook, the CEO of a biotechnology company called Cenentech, nibbled on blueberry skyr cake and sipped tea, as did her friends.

"The embargo idea may work," Cook said, "but I already had my people talk to the Nigerian president, Adeyemi. He's not on board. Hughes's new trade deal with him is making both countries a lot of money."

"Our counteroffer on OPEC and mining was far superior to Hughes's," Blair said, puzzled. He sat erect on the circular white couch that enclosed the three of them. He couldn't understand why Adeyemi wouldn't take the offer, as corrupt as Nigeria was.

Cook reached for another small piece of cake on the oval glass table in front of them. "President Adeyemi made a deal with the Hughes administration. An article released by BBC News three months ago confirmed the arrest of twelve corrupt Nigerian officials. The Nigerian government was funded back billions of dollars from this corruption, with the help of FBI operatives personally sent by Hughes."

"POTUS has Adeyemi in her pocket," Robertson said.

"Not only that," Cook said, "but that human-trip-to-Mars thing she naively campaigned about quite possibly could come true. Nigeria and the United States, right now as we speak, are building a vessel. They have found new tantalums in Nigeria that this spacecraft is being manufactured from."

"I know," Robertson said. "They're not breaking any deals for anybody. Too much prestige and dignity involved."

"It might be time for a regime change," Blair said.

Everyone slowly nodded.

"Our next order of business is relocating the ESM project," Blair said, looking from one face to the other.

"I'll undergo this," Robertson said. "I know the perfect spot to put this black project."

Blair appreciated that most presidents of the United States did what they were told. They would lecture elegantly and convince the American people that it wasn't their fault but was the fault of the other parties or Congress that their proposal hadn't been implemented. Blair giggled to himself. *Obama never closed GTMO, and W. Bush attacked Iraq for practically no reason. Carter never got those hostages released, and Ike never had that summit with the Russians, because we told the Russians the Americans were coming to spy on their country. All these things went into motion with our interest at heart.*

Sometimes things didn't work for their benefit, however. They hadn't managed to assassinate Castro but had gotten Che. Blair snickered to himself again. In his estimation, if his assassins came after you, there was a 99 percent chance you were going to die.

Their organization, Ides of March, had gotten rid of Diem, Hammarskjöld, Kennedy, and many others. Blair felt this Nigerian regime change was insignificant in the grand scheme of things. He just wondered how Hughes was going to react. Falling in line was all she could do. Ides of March was a society too potent for any president, especially this black lady, this true-freedom-for-everybody dreamer. *We have too many people everywhere.* Blair sniggered to himself again.

If President Hughes had been facing him now, he would have quoted to her one of her addresses to the American people: "You can't stop the very momentum of history."

FIRESIDE TWEETS

China–United States Relations

I believe we can accomplish a lot despite territorial issues in the South China Sea, arms to Taiwan, cyberespionage, and trade policies. We can do great things with reducing nuclear proliferation and climate change and tighten sanctions on Iran, Syria, and North Korea. We argue too much on small things because we have so little of the great to conceal. Too many of us are doing great stuff in small ponds; it's time to break limits and boundaries and head to Mars. Let's make it happen!

—Sarah Hughes

CHAPTER 8

Friday

9:00 a.m.

President Hughes had managed to accomplish almost everything she'd campaigned about. Bailey thought of Hughes's stance on gun control. Executive order 14168 demanded all gun owners in every state be evaluated every year. She was pro-choice and supported laws ensuring abortion rights. Hughes did not speak much about LGBTQ rights, except to say, "They have the right to marry in every state, and I believe in 'Don't Ask, Don't Tell.'" She had supported and signed Congress's Minimum Wage Fairness Act a month ago, which had raised the minimum wage to sixteen dollars per hour.

Then there was Congress's proposed legislation geared toward the top 10 percent of the rich. The law ensured no more tax loopholes, such as using shell companies and tax havens, avoiding capital gains taxes, and evading estate taxes. She had signed the bill, making such loopholes officially illegal. She continued the Dodd-Frank Act and argued endlessly the point of regulating banks.

She had no sympathy for Section 8 housing, unless one physically worked for it. She wasn't in favor of the wealthy circumnavigating taxes, calling it corporate welfare. She made it clear that she was a president for the middle class, and she detested oligarchies.

Hughes put her head in her hands and then continued to stare at the screens. Her eyes seemed to water as she listened to BBC and MSNBC news chatter about the Nigerian president, Musa Adeyemi.

Boko Haram, a jihadist organization, had taken credit for the assassination of President Adeyemi. Adeyemi and Hughes had been friends since she won the presidential primaries and caucuses.

She sipped on some white zin with Secretary of Defense Leon Cohen, while everyone else had coffee or water.

All the usual individuals gathered in the room around the rectangular mahogany table whenever a crisis came about, including Chief of Staff McCarthy, DNI Clark, and newly appointed fleet admiral Douglas Dewey.

Bailey felt like a fly on the wall, as he usually did. He stood by the door in the basement conference room under the West Wing, making sure the meeting wasn't interrupted.

Hughes spoke, eyeballing each individual in the room except Bailey. "Congress voted to overturn my executive order to penalize all American corporations who outsource. I tried to stop most countries, particularly China, from lending us greenbacks. Buying US debt is a low risk, making our deficit an ongoing cycle. American companies were going to make a lot of moolah in trade deals with Nigeria and go to Mars under my administration. Now this." She was quiet for a second, scrutinizing everyone again, and then whispered loudly enough for all to hear, "Holy Joe! It's as if someone is propeller-washing me."

"I don't mean to raise your ire," McCarthy said to Hughes, "but Vice President Shehu Jonathan, now the president of Nigeria, is freezing all deals with the United States until the investigation of this assassination is sorted out by his SSS."

"And they rejected our assistance," Hughes said, knowing already but wanting to hear the inevitable.

McCarthy and Cohen did not utter a word; they only nodded.

"We're going to investigate anyway," Hughes said. "I want Hellbender on this one."

"Ma'am," Cohen said, "he's FBI and has never dealt with foreign affairs of this nature."

Hughes glanced at Dewey and then nodded an okay to tell their story.

Dewey cleared his throat. "Hellbender is also part of the NSA's black op, unbeknownst to everyone in this room except me and the president. Now you guys know, exposing him more."

"This is of the highest security," Hughes said, peeking at Bailey. "This can't go farther than this room."

"Will he be able to handle both cases simultaneously?" Clark asked.

"He's done it before," Dewey said. "His record is unblemished. D. B. Cooper's body was found in the Columbia River with one hundred ninety-four thousand dollars in twenties still strapped to him. Teeth and bone fragments of Jimmy Hoffa were found in a scrap-metal landfill in Honshu, Japan. These 1970 deaths were Hellbender's first cases. From then on, we knew he was extraordinary."

Cohen smiled. "Then he surely knows who assassinated Kennedy."

"Some things are classified," Dewey said somberly, deleting the frown from Cohen's visage. "Furthermore, what I just told you is classified."

"I want an update on this periodically, ducky," Hughes said. In her slim-fit stone-gray business suit, she blended with the attitudes of everyone as they filed out of the room.

Bailey perceived that she was pissed when she walked past him and didn't give him a peep.

In 1990, Fleet Admiral Dewey had led aircraft carriers and battleships, including the USS *Dwight D. Eisenhower*, *Independence*, *Missouri*, and *Wisconsin*, in the Gulf War, codenamed Operation Desert Shield and Operation Desert Storm. He'd commanded strikes in the 2001 Afghanistan War, deploying B-1 Lancer bombers and C-130 Hercules cargo planes against the Taliban forces. In the 2003 invasion of Iraq, he'd directed the first strikes with seventy thousand marines, four destroyers, and two submarines in the Persian Gulf. In 2011, he'd ordered eleven ships and F-16 jets to bomb military targets in Libya.

Dewey was as famous as Hughes. Bailey liked to believe most Americans appreciated what Hughes believed in. She explosively expressed her convictions in unalienable rights; freedom of speech, the press, and religion; separation of church and state; the right of due process; and environmental justice and against inequality. The *Washington Post* and *Newsweek* had put President Hughes's politics on par with those of Bill Clinton and Nancy Pelosi.

As she already had been legendary for being the twenty-five-year-old female African American mayor of New York City, it hadn't been a surprise when she won the presidency by a landslide. She'd lost the popular vote in only two states: Alaska and Texas. She'd won the electoral vote, something she wanted to get rid of, in every state except South Carolina. The media affirmed they hadn't seen the likes of that since Ronald Reagan. That alone acknowledged what America thought of Madam President Sarah Jefferson Hughes.

Patriotic Americans who closely followed politics saw Dewey as similarly noteworthy. Many news articles associated him with Dwight Eisenhower and George S. Patton. The public saw him as a stern but eccentric old man with a lot of spunk and guts. Obviously, militarism was his dictum, and it was rumored that he had seen a UFO once, which made him more paranoid that the United States was being infiltrated by terrorists or invaded. The Republicans saw him as a megastar, a Captain America—they loved him.

Bailey suspected if Hughes had had an envious bone in her body for anyone, Dewey would have been the one. Bailey had heard her whisper many times that Dewey was an imperialist and a loose cannon that needed to be watched. Through popular demand, in Bailey's eyes, she had been forced to appoint him fleet admiral with the consent of Congress, making history. The last living fleet admiral had been Chester W. Nimitz, who'd been appointed in 1944.

The nomination had boosted her already soaring approval rating.

FIRESIDE TWEETS

State of the US Stock Exchange

I may sound like a broken record, but the economy is doing great, with unemployment dropping steadily and job growth. Big companies feel my regulations stifle reinvesting and hiring. On the whole, tax cuts only help cooperate America and don't trickle down to the middle class enough. We need young companies—like mine—to attract investors with great ideas so the company value will rise. Supply and demand. The test of our progress is not in adding more to the abundance of those who have much but in providing enough for those who have little. If we follow this, America is headed in the right direction.

—Sarah Hughes

CHAPTER 9

10:00 p.m.

McCarthy and other advisers told Bailey not to be politically divisive. He was not to show any political influences on Russian-American bilateral relationships by virtue. In other words, he was not to say anything; he was just to be a host. One reporter did ask him what he was doing there and if he was a partygoer.

"Yes, of course, and eyewitness," Bailey responded.

"Wasn't it like the president to be escorted by the USSS?" the media wrote, but the criticism didn't go further than that because Hughes stole the show.

Bailey had never seen the president in a dress, nor had she ever paraded her legs in front of so many cameras before, unless a photographer snuck up on her from behind, like when she went jogging in the summertime. At that black-tie event, she wore a slim-fit royal-blue skirt suit displaying her shape and her earth-yellow legs, and her toes were visible in open-toed stilettos. The press hadn't known her toes existed until that day, nor had Ivankov.

It was an undersized state dinner by presidential standards but sizeable by media measures. Countless photos were taken of Ivankov; his wife, Yelena; and Hughes on the North Portico and in the Entrance Hall and Blue Room. Olivia Ravi, Hughes's personal photographer, took pleasure in photographing the presidents in the Yellow Oval Room and, ushered by Bailey, descending the Grand Staircase to the Grand Foyer.

After the US Marine Band played "President's Own," "Hail to the Chief," the national anthem, and "Gosudarstvenny Gimn Rossiyskoy Federatsii," Bailey escorted everyone to the State Dining Room. With the delightful music of live jazz pianist Keith Javrett, both presidents, numerous dignitaries, some members of the US Congress, and the executive branch and their wives ate a four-course meal.

Hughes was enchanting in her jokes and speeches. She had studied Russian culture and Slavic mythology, folklore, ballet, and football. As the Russian and American press told it, she impressed Vadim Ivankov and his wife on their first encounter.

The Washington Monument was lit up like a snow cone as Bailey glanced out the floor-to-ceiling windows late that night. He and Hughes were alone in the solarium—probably the only place in that house where one could be alone, Bailey knew. She had told him not to go home but to meet her there after the dinner and private talks with the Russian president. The press didn't know about it, but his colleagues were going to spread rumors. He could hear them talking already.

The light was faint as they sat on a settee together. She held a full glass of Dominio de Pingus, and told him that she wouldn't bite; she just wanted to talk.

"Do you want me to make a statement?" Hughes asked.

"I don't think the press thinks I'll be occupying the second-floor residence. No need."

They continued to look out the window at the Washington, DC, lights. *Like fireflies*, he thought.

"You pretty much had every eye on you," he said. He watched her sip her scarlet wine; he could smell the richness. "Is that a gift from Ivankov?"

She blinked as if roused from some deep thought, nodded, and said, "The souvenir I gave him was for his wife. She adores American jazz. I myself can't stand it. I'm Sisters of Mercy all the way."

She wasn't lying. He had to endure her music every time she practiced her grappling.

"If you don't mind me asking," Bailey said, "with all this gift giving, how were the negotiations?"

She sighed. "We have many interests and conflicts in Syria, Ukraine, and Iran. It's always 'Provide or seize' in Eastern Europe.

"North Korea owes Russia billions. Russia is building a pipeline through North Korea into South Korea, relieving North Korea of all debt and giving gas to South Korea, killing two birds with one stone. I suggested to Ivankov that he stop allowing North Korean immigrants in and halt the pipeline. I also suggested we could ease our own sanctions on Russia. Then we'd let them be part of the Human Mission to Mars project in Nigeria maybe. He said he'd agree to that, minus the immigrants and plus our leaving the Syria situation alone. Granted, only if I still have control of the project. Sounds promising, I told him."

"Madam," Bailey said carefully, "no disrespect, but I think he's taking advantage of you. How much do you think Ivankov really admires you? His eyes were admiring you all night."

She laughed. "Was he admiring me? I think he was just making you and everyone else jealous." She then gave a pondering expression. "He said that I was well versed in world affairs and that my heart was in the right place but that I was a bit naive when it came to reading leaders. I felt he listened too much to the American press. I think he meant that no matter what, some things are nonnegotiable."

Bailey loosened his bow tie as they both sat more comfortably on the settee. He hadn't expected to stay this long or have this conversation, but there he was. He was there to be the president's therapist. *This is some serious overtime.* He laughed to himself. *Yeah, this is definitely overtime.*

"You're a virtuous person, Madam President," he said. "Sort of makes you a loner. Most world leaders are conniving and erode human dignity."

"My parents taught me the only ones who endure suppression are the resilient. The world is brutal, they said, so we have to be brutal with this." She pointed to her head. "They can't take that from you." She stared at him, playing with her wineglass.

He looked down, thinking of what to say. "Not on my watch, but they could exterminate you, and then—"

"Nah, they'd make me a martyr." She paused again, drinking, reflecting. "Besides, Ivankov said I wouldn't go out that way. He said—jokingly, but I think he was serious—that as soon as I get into a relationship, I'll lose my power to lead."

"A bit of a chauvinist he is. Not surprised."

"No. He sounded like a clairvoyant. Funny thing—I almost believed him."

They both leaned back on the sofa. Their heads were close. He could smell the rich wine on her breath. If they were going to kiss, now was as good a time as any.

Someone knocked on the door, and they both straightened up.

"Come in!" Hughes shouted over her shoulder.

One of Bailey's men, part of his SADP detail, stuck his head into the room. "Madam, you have Prime Minister Osborne on the phone."

Four o'clock in the morning in England, and the prime minister of the United Kingdom had to call now. Well, Bailey's night was over. He knew he was going to hear an earful from his coworkers, who would say he'd been smooching with the president, though no such action had taken place.

Bailey thought more about the meeting Ivankov and Hughes had had after dinner. If the pipeline deal, which was not only for South Korea, was halted, it might stall North Korea's nuclear weapons program. That would tighten Russian sanctions, making the DPRK still in deep debt. Then, of course, there were other issues. For one, Ivankov believed China wasn't doing their part in placing harsher restrictions.

China controlled much of the DPRK's foreign trade. Hughes had informed Ivankov that she would negotiate with China to stop selling DPRK coal. For Russia to join the Human Mission to Mars, or HMM, project, reducing sanctions and leaving Syria alone, unless they had to chase a terrorist cell, wasn't enough to convince Ivankov.

To have Russia fully compliant with stronger sanctions on the DPRK, she had to gain control again of the Human Mission to Mars project.

The prime minister's call was definitely going to be about the HMM project, Bailey knew. Prime Minister Eric Osborne adored President Hughes the way the American people did. He even boasted that it was great to talk to true ancestry. Hughes's father was half black and half white and a descendant of Eston Hemings, the child of Sally Hemings, from the line of Founding Father Thomas Jefferson. Bailey thought, *Let's see if this descendant can convince Nigeria and the world to continue the project.*

The discovery of her lineage had not only made President Hughes a legend but also strengthened the Me Too movement and created more girl-power engagements across the country. The leader of the Me Too movement and many American celebrities had mentioned that the president had never recognized them or spoken on their behalf.

Bailey figured Hughes would not focus on any one specific group. She was the president of the United States of America, not an activist, but she descried all activism.

FIRESIDE TWEETS

On Bail Reform

Sounds like a state-level resolution like a stand-your-ground law or castle doctrine. We need to have stronger rehabilitation programs. I support the New Jersey bail-reform law, the Speedy Trial Act, aimed to decrease jail populations, saving city costs. A judge determines whether to release or detain a defendant. We must remember the Kalief Browder case. This should absolutely be exclusively for petty crimes. An affluent person can easily pay his or her bail, whereas an underprivileged person spends years in jail. What's sauce for the goose is sauce for the gander.

—Sarah Hughes

CHAPTER 10

Wednesday Evening

The president had traveled extensively during the first four months of her presidency. Bailey felt it was like traveling with a rock star or athlete. Commercials for her software company had been the start of her recognition; her face and her company name, Computer Systems Tech, or CST, had traveled to people first. According to *Forbes* magazine, CST, a globally growing company that distributed new wireless energy and holograms, would be worth $1 billion before the year's end.

Starting the day after the inauguration, Hughes and Vice President Adams, either solo or together, had visited all fifty states and Puerto Rico. Their message, like their campaign, was about transparency, equality, renewed self-determination, and supporting the middle class.

Hughes lectured at universities; spoke on television shows, at press conferences, and in interviews; and conversed at the Alfalfa Club about the Green New Deal, the federal budget, embryonic stem-cell research, drug-control policies, and renewed sanctions against North Korea.

Hughes preached intensively on foreign and domestic terrorism and had created executive orders to expand Guantanamo Bay, the Pentagon, and Camp David and ordered Predator airstrikes around the world.

Bailey had flown with her aboard Air Force One to meet presidents and prime ministers in Brazil, Mexico, Israel, Canada, and Japan.

Hughes had nominated federal judge Joshua Moretti, who'd gained a reputation for being opinionated, feisty, firm, and fair and showing tough love. That had led to the first thwarted assassination attempt on Hughes's life. A chauvinistic man affiliated with ANU, who loathed the judge, had conspired to eradicate Hughes at the G20 summit in New Delhi, India.

The USSS had arrested the ANU individual, who had been following Hughes for a week, at Indira Gandhi International Airport and found an L115A3 long-range rifle with telescopic sighting in his suitcase, therefore ending his conspiracy against the president.

Bailey had attained information on the man from the Mossad and SIS, who had been following the sniper for years, leading to the arrest. Bailey bet Hughes had thanked the chiefs of state of Israel and the United Kingdom for their intelligence at the G20 conference.

In the sky again, in the middle of the North Atlantic, Air Force One flew above a brewing storm. Through the porthole, Bailey watched a couple of fluorescent-blue lightning flashes below. He was dozing off while listening to Charles Mingus and evaluating the thunderstorm, in one of the many Secret Service quarters, when a communication came in. His videophone buzzed, snapping him to attention.

"Sorry to bother you at this hour," Deputy Director Giuliani said on a small video screen. "I believe Hellbender has some crucial information. He says he hasn't concluded his investigation, but he knows who Duran is and who conspired in the assassination of President Adeyemi."

"So soon?" Bailey asked, surprised. "And you can confirm these findings? I'm about to interrupt a meeting the president is having. If this is concrete, she wants this right away."

"It's solid. Hellbender requested to talk to the president personally."

"Give me five or ten minutes, and I'll call you back." Bailey sighed and then moved to the main conference room.

Though Bailey knew the significance of the meeting taking place, he interrupted it on the notion of crucial current events. DNI Clark had just finished briefing Hughes on a secret operation called ESM. Bailey knew about a lot of clandestine operations, but he didn't know about that one. He even knew about Project Safeguard, which was so covert that even the president's closest cabinet members knew nothing about it. *It's true that if you want to keep a secret, the fewer people you tell the better.*

After reporting to Wise, the body man, his highly sensitive and important reason for disrupting POTUS, Bailey was escorted into the main conference room.

Bailey leaned over and whispered in Hughes's ear, "Hellbender has some pressing information on the Adeyemi debacle and wants an audience with you."

Hughes turned to Bailey with a serious look and then realized it was him and grinned. "Meet me in my office. I'll be there in two minutes."

As Bailey left the conference room, he already figured who wasn't coming to the private office meeting. Probably none of her advisers, he thought, and to his surprise, not even McCarthy made it to the classified engagement.

After a few minutes, Hughes sat behind her replica Resolute desk in her office, watching Bailey set up videoconferencing at an opposite wall. He opened mahogany wall panels, exposing an enormous monitor. The director of the National Security Agency and commander of the US Cyber Command, George R. Jacobs, sat on a cocoa-brown leather chair to the right of the president's desk. DNI Clark and Bailey soon sat on a couch off to the side as everyone intensely stared at the screen.

"Good afternoon, Madam President," Giuliani said, his face filling the screen. "Sorry—I mean evening. It should be evening for you guys. To begin, as you already know, Hellbender has some crucial information."

"Okay, let's not keep us in suspense," Hughes said. "Put Kid Foreshadow on."

"Yes, Madam President," Giuliani said, removing himself, and Hellbender then filled the display.

Hellbender, in a ruffled yellow shirt and tie, went through cluttered papers in front of him. An open *PC Gamer* magazine sat to the side.

Bailey watched Hughes smile as Hellbender spoke with his eyes down, looking at his jumbled notes, which made sense only to him.

"Arthur Duran, whose real name is John Birch, is a forty-year retired CIA operative and now far-right activist and hacker. I've discovered his many forged accounts. He raids banks and receives money from a man named Brett McMahon, who is a retired bodyguard for an Ian Blair. It's a considerable amount—millions of dollars. This bodyguard has given millions to the AIP, the Tea Party movement, crime cartel associations around the world, and Wahhabi ideology organizations, like al-Shabaab, al-Qaeda, and ISWAP."

"Now that we have names," Jacobs said, "do we know more about Brett McMahon? His occupation now? His motives?"

The screen flickered, and they heard part of what Hellbender said. "Know Brett's occupation. And don't know his motives, except the obvious that he supports radical groups."

Jacobs had to ask twice, as Hellbender couldn't hear him, and the screen glimmered again. "Who is Ian Blair?"

"Ian Blair is an economist, part head of international organizations, and CEO of Hoffro Holdings, headquartered in France," Hellbender answered.

"Hipper-dipper, Foreshadow," Hughes said. "If we have any more information we'll transfer through secure lines, all reet."

Giuliani and Hellbender nodded, and the screen went dark.

Jacobs, using his laptop, brought up information from the internet on Ian Blair. "Blair has been CEO and chairman of the board of Hoffro since 2012. It's an American pharmaceutical company with businesses in Europe, the Middle East, and Africa. He has a bachelor of science degree in electrical engineering and graduated from Harvard Business School with a master's in business administration. He spent six years in the US Army, finishing with a rank of captain. He developed database projects for the CIA and was named one of the One Hundred Most Inspiring Leaders by *Entrepreneur* magazine."

Hughes smirked. "I wonder what his interests are in Nigeria." She spoke to herself more than to anybody else.

"We'll have to collect info on this Brett McMahon," Jacobs said. "Then connect the dots on McMahon and possibly Birch, alias Duran, to President Adeyemi's assassination."

"George, Pete, I need a complete report on Blair and McMahon," Hughes said. "Joe, look into Birch." She looked around the room. "Guys, I needed this yesterday."

Everyone looked at each other and dispersed.

"I need to flap lips with you for a second," Hughes said, eyeing Bailey.

"Ma'am," Bailey said, stopping at the door behind everyone who'd left.

From a cabinet, Hughes pulled out two glasses and a bottle of cabernet sauvignon. She poured a half glass each of the red wine. "I know you're on duty," she said. "I won't tell. It's just a little hair of the dog."

"No, thank you. I'll pass. Really," Bailey said.

"Suit yourself. It's really good giggle water. Taste." She waved a glass in the air after taking a sip. He shook his head, looking at her seriously.

Leaning on the front of her desk with her arms folded, she held the wineglass in hand. "So what do you think? You think this could be inside work? Things like this are always inside affairs."

With arms folded, pacing, Bailey thought hard before responding. "Could be anybody. Your closest friends, family, me. Washington is actually a big place when it comes to inside jobs. Right now, the good thing is, we have names."

"You think the very organization feeding us these names could be turncoats?"

"The FBI? Hellbender? You have to trust somebody, ma'am."

Hughes stared at Bailey for a moment, but to him, it seemed like forever before she spoke again. "I trust Kid Foreshadow, and I trust you, Joseph." She looked away at the wood-paneled walls and sipped her wine.

INTERVIEW WITH TREVOR NOAH

Police Brutality on African Americans

During my presidential campaign and after my inauguration, I visited problematic police departments. I've already signed an executive order on this crisis. Every state police department requires trainees to go through special psychological training before they become officers. This police reform order is reinstated every five years. It's called the DeGruy Doctrine. It basically teaches empathy toward other races. It examines why some individuals have contempt for others and cognitive-dissonance behaviors. The soul always knows how to heal itself. The challenge is to silence the mind.

—Sarah Hughes

CHAPTER 11

Canada, Sunday

5:00 p.m.

The granite manor in York Mills, Toronto, Ontario, sat on a hill overlooking a freshwater alpine lake. Of Ian Blair's many living rooms, this one had a veranda that led to a pool area with a waterfall. Cook and Robertson sat on a white couch, while Blair sat on an armchair facing them with his legs crossed. Blair's and Robertson's wives resided in the dining room, chatting and waiting for the private chef to finish dinner. Cook's husband had passed five years ago.

"I've been exposed." Blair began the reunion.

His counterparts sighed heavily while sipping their tea slowly.

"How do you know this?" Robertson asked. "What happened?"

"There was a breach in one of our black projects. The regime change in Nigeria is being investigated," Blair said. "On the president's flight to England, my name came up in a report."

"She has meddled in our affairs long enough," Cook said. "Our companies are quivering all over the globe because of her policies."

"This has been going on far too long," Robertson said. "We anticipated this long before she became president."

"If this keeps up for four years," Cook said, "the West, the free world, will lose its hold on imperialism. It's actually happening now as we speak, like a virus."

"No more Green New Deal," Robertson said boisterously. "An end to gun control, banking reform, ungodly agnosticism, health care for all, socialism, and progressive ideas."

"POTUS is creating her own new world order," Cook said. "This nig—we need to remain firm to the conservative ways of Christian values, prolife, minimal government, and capitalism."

"We sound like true far-right ideologists." Blair sat back in his seat. "Are we getting old in our ways?"

"Never." Robertson smiled. "We'll initiate Project Death Storm and rid ourselves of this plague."

"Yes, our matrix networks are far and wide," Blair said. "If we do this, we will set things in motion again in historic proportions."

Cook looked at the other two and exhaled noisily, as if a heavy weight were upon her shoulders. "Capitalism could be lost. Our ideologies gone astray. We all could be exposed. If there is a one percent chance of this, it has to be eradicated. There's no other choice. This must be done in the first quarter of her presidency."

"It's decided then," Blair said, raising his teacup. The others elevated their cups as well. "Death Storm."

Death Storm could last a week or years, Blair knew. Assassination of a prominent figure was always grueling, never cut-and-dried. It was tedious and arduous because some media, conspiracy theorists, and curiosity seekers wanted to investigate too much, even when there was no conspiracy.

IM, Ides of March, had kept controversial secrets long before he was initiated into the sect after college, and he was sure those secrets would be kept long after he was gone. IM was in the business of making history. Some considered the cult malevolent, and others thought it agreeable. He thought it necessary. There was no justice or inequality in the mind of the organization, only correctness and pyramid order.

Pyramid order, which had been created in 1119 and gone global in 1845, was structured for the elite and the strongest minds. He, his constituents, scientists, and their families were at the top; celebrities were in the middle; and the public, the sheep, were at the bottom. Blair was prideful in knowing IM was the octopus, with tentacles that had reached the Knights Templar, which had transformed into the Order of the Solar Temple, the Black Hand, Ordo Templi Orientis, and the Bilderberg Group. Their families were appreciative in knowing they'd saved the United States on Jekyll Island and constructed the Federal Reserve.

Death Storm was going to work. If they wanted someone to go away, he or she went away, Blair thought.

60 MINUTES WITH ANDERSON COOPER

On the Economy

What my administration has done to help the largest-GDP economy in the world is simply open more global trade. I'm not an expert in macroeconomics, but having easy access to education, like learning the automation process of a computerized world, makes human capital rise. The cyber industry has made the world more manageable in merchandising, and that equals connectivity, productivity, and higher wages, resulting in a rise in living standards. My administration has also prioritized the maintenance and rebuilding of roads, buildings, and bridges. We are now trying to make big companies sitting on trillions of dollars and bonuses create more jobs so working folks can spend more. I call it simply mathematics.

—Sarah Hughes

CHAPTER 12

Friday

10:15 p.m.

Paramount leader, core leader, and president of the People's Republic of China, Xi Jinping, had visited the United States many times. He was scheduled to visit this time for three days to discuss foreign affairs in the Oval Office. The media reported that the engagement was about new bilateral relations, cyberwarfare, trade policies, climate change, and the South China Sea.

Jinping actually stayed for a week. The press alleged Hughes had wowed him and gotten the best of him in negotiations. In truth, Bailey knew, she just wanted Jinping to get on board with the HMM project.

The only thing she captivated him with was a gala dinner banquet on his last day. Dialogue in the Oval Office, both private and in front of cameras, was indeed about cyberwarfare and the South China Sea. Those issues went nowhere. What the cameras did not see was Hughes's quarreling about China's selling coal to the DPRK.

"Hold on," Hughes told Bailey as everyone left the buff-colored West Sitting Hall. Bailey nodded as senior advisers Peter Steelman and McCarthy and Secretary of State John Powell filed out of the vestibule.

It was becoming familiar for her to tell him to stay back. That day, Jinping's last day, Hughes had nattered to Jinping privately for three hours.

Then she'd talked to her advisers for two hours after. *Now, at this hour, tonight she wants me to hold on most likely to shoot the breeze.*

"How do you think the body language was between me and the general sectary?" Hughes asked, pacing.

"I thought you were yourself," Bailey answered. "Actually, Xi seemed a bit nervous."

"That's what I thought," she responded in excitement. "Kev and everyone kept saying I seemed apprehensive this time in negotiating with Xi."

"Well, I think we're all a little anxious to get this done."

"Xi said he can only guarantee a cease-fire on missile testing in international waters. I told him if the missile testing continued and he couldn't give me the coal deal, we'd cut them from the program. Not the deal I wanted, because we would like China involved in the HMM project. Now I don't know."

"I think China wants to be part of this project," Bailey said. "To be in concert with history. He wouldn't have traveled all this way to not see some sort of deal go through."

"So do you want a little liquid courage? I won't tell the big cheese. Wait a minute—I'm your head honcho." She smiled.

"No, ma'am, really. I'm good."

She put a hand out for him to sit on an artichoke-colored couch. "Will you keep me company for a second while I pour myself some giggle water?"

"Certainly. I serve at the pleasure of the president."

Hughes displayed discomfort across her face. He knew she heard that line time and again. After pouring herself a half glass of red wine, she sat on the couch across from him.

"You think if I were a fella, they'd say I was anxious?" Hughes stared at him solemnly.

"Can't say, Madam President." Bailey gave a panicky grin.

Taking a sip, she took a long pause before speaking. "Any new development on the ANU case? I heard you Joe Blows have a briefing for me tomorrow. Can you brief me before the brief so I can go to bed knowing what to expect in the morning?"

"For one," Bailey said, crossing his legs, "you're going to get a lot more details on the suspects. One person—someone I don't think is going to get a lot of attention at tomorrow's briefing—caught my attention."

She got up from the couch to plop down next to him, careful not to spill her drink. "Who is it that you feel the need to take a gander at?"

"It's the CEO of Hoffro Holdings, Ian Blair," Bailey answered. "He could possibly be behind everything. I believe he's untouchable."

"Why do you think that?"

"His hands are everywhere." Bailey sighed. "Blair has supported Democrats and Republicans; has defense contracts with the CIA, projects with the Pentagon, and family ties with the Rockefellers; knows former president Vladimir Putin; and has business ties with China in computer sciences."

Hughes took a taste of wine, placed the glass on a table, and leaned in closer to Bailey. "Nobody's invulnerable. I'll sleep on that. It'll also make me sleep better knowing what you think your friends and the media are saying about us."

He took a long pause. "They don't say much." Then he gave a smirk. "You play the convincing game well, and you know it. I think they all know I'm the chauffeur."

She smiled. "Not many people know I was almost hitched once. A Joe Blow from the Third Brigade's Tenth Mountain Division."

She paused for a long while, staring at him, pleading with her eyes for him to say, "So what happened?"

"We were shot at by snipers on foot patrol," she said. "He was hit. I haven't told anybody that story in a long while."

He watched her pick up her drink and down the rest of it before he asked, "Do I remind you of him?"

Hughes fiddled with the empty glass. "No," she said shyly. "It was back when I attended college. I was extremely patriotic then. I loved the marines' academy, combat, and the smell of artillery. My parents taught me to be nationalistic.

"Now I'm more into technology-savvy, nonpartisan, clandestine Casanova cloud-walkers. Like you." She quickly kissed him on the forehead and then on the cheek. She stood up and sighed. "Let me retire before something happens and your unit really does have something to flap their lips about. Like your disappearance for a couple of hours or something of that nature."

He wanted to say, "I can disappear for a couple of hours. We can tell those fools something."

Instead, he said, "Yes, ma'am." He felt the president watch him as he left the hall.

INTERVIEW WITH OPRAH WINFREY

How to Improve Affordable Housing

This country was against home ownership for minorities from the start. In the '60s, it was called redlining. The immediate cure is rent control. I believe in the Mitchell-Lama Housing Program for middle-income families. My administration is working to spread this program across the nation. For communities who have lost this program, my administration has been toiling tiresomely to reinstate it.

—Sarah Hughes

CHAPTER 13

Saudi Arabia, Friday One Week Later

10:00 a.m.

Bailey had wanted more than a week to set up a detail to protect President Hughes in Saudi Arabia. For weeks, the president had rehearsed a speech about the withdrawal of troops in the Middle East and America's stance on the Arab world. This time, the president didn't want to travel the conventional way. Usually, it took the USSS two to three weeks to clear any country as safe for a visit by the president. They'd approved that excursion in a week. It was more like a surprise stopover, Bailey thought.

He had sent agents on Saturday to Al-Yamamah University in Riyadh. He then had gone himself on Monday, before the rest of his detail on Wednesday. Collaborating with the Mabahith was always nerve-wracking, Bailey believed. Though the Kingdom of Saudi Arabia was excited for the president's arrival, Bailey still felt untrusting toward the Middle East in general.

The head of the General Intelligence Directorate, or GID, Khalid bin Sultan, was accommodating and enthusiastic that Hughes was coming. That was what scared him. Bailey had told Khalid and his central squad, besides the king, not to tell anyone the president was coming until the night before. There were about eighty men in the tight GID circle; Bailey wondered how many of them were stoolies.

Riyadh was going to be 102 degrees that day, with clear blue skies. Bailey knew most of the agents would be sporting shades. They locked down the college, particularly the main auditorium building, only allowing in a select group of three hundred students, delegates, and the royal family. King Fahd Branch Road, the main highway to the university, was secured for the day, forcing pedestrians to use alternate routes and causing traffic in other areas. They also had a straight shot to the Eskan Village Compound if they needed an emergency evacuation. Motorcade to Marine One to Air Force One was their method of transportation for escape. The Gerald R. Ford–class aircraft carrier sat in the Persian Gulf to provide more backup if needed.

King Salman and Prince Muhammad arrived first. The royal family and their advisers were greeted by cheers from a crowd of about four hundred individuals lining both sides of a pathway to the entrance of the college grounds.

Positioning himself by a railing on one side of the lane, Bailey scrutinized the gathering of heavily robed individuals. He didn't like the idea that he didn't have thawb-wearing undercovers in that crowd, as he had inside the building. He especially didn't like the idea that Khalid was in control of the outside detail. To make the trip successful, he had to trust other countries' surveillance. Winning the confidence of other countries made apprehending spies, cartels, and terrorists easier.

Second to appear, from two black Chevrolet Suburbans in another motorcade, were some of the White House press corps. Last, after the decoy first car and the exit of some Secret Service members, was the Beast. With the necessary ring of agents surrounding Cadillac One, Hughes emerged, followed by Curt Reich, assistant to and speechwriter for the president.

As Hughes made her way to the congregated pathway, working the rope line, an individual in the swarm pretending to take a photo fell over the barrier. When the young man stood up, instead of taking a picture, he waved a nine-millimeter. Someone in the crowd screamed.

The boy must have been senseless, Bailey thought. That moment was what he had been trained for. Bailey whipped into action. It was what he lived for: to protect the president of the United States of America with his life.

Before Bailey or other agents could grab the kid, the youngster fired. It was a miracle that the gun misfired and a greater marvel that Hughes moved so swiftly—not to retreat but to advance before the Secret Service grabbed her.

With three martial-arts hand movements, President Hughes disarmed the assailant. Some agents grabbed the assaulter and Hughes and separated them in seconds. Bailey, who was eight feet away from the action, wondered if the crowd was flabbergasted about the goon or that Hughes had attacked the assaulter—probably both.

It wasn't over, as more shrieks sounded from the dispersing jamboree. Another assailant fired from behind Bailey, hitting an agent in the back. Bailey jumped over the railing and gave chase as the perp took off running. His leap over the guardrail injured two civilians, but he managed to run down the gunman. Using Systema tactics, Bailey dislodged the assailant's weapon and then slammed him facedown on the ground. Not only did you have to chase a criminal, but when you caught him, you had to apprehend him, and that was work. He was glad his everyday morning jogs paid off. *Cardio, everyone,* Bailey thought, reminiscing on his training. All agents had to do cardio.

"Clear." A voice reverberated in his coiled-tube earpiece.

After another agent came and secured his aggressor, Bailey spoke into his mic. "Is the Lioness away?"

"No, the Little Lioness is still here, in the stagecoach," the lead agent, Oscar, said in his ear.

What! Bailey shouted in his skull. *What is she still doing here?*

In the aftermath, Bailey assessed there had been six shooters, three shooters had died, and four agents had been shot. POTUS stayed to make her speech. It was crazy, Bailey thought, but the press, the House of Saud, and the Middle East ate it up. After surviving her second assassination attempt, she gave her speech about peace in the Middle East. Hughes gave her oration on the Al-Yamamah campus, in the grand auditorium, in front of an audience of thousands.

"We will not let the minority of extremists deter us from the goal of peace," she said. "Peace is not feeble. I believe it's easy to hate our enemy and never forgive but hard to forgive our enemy eventually to love. It's easy to destroy but hard to build. I see strength in love. But do not confuse kindness for weakness.

"These proxy cold wars have to end. We, the United States, have to be the first example to show that power of peace."

She went on a lengthy discourse about Israel, Palestine, and Hezbollah sitting down at a table to negotiate a final agreement of territory. She had confidence that Libya, Syria, Yemen, and Iraq would grow into stable, flourishing governments.

"Hopefully the Sunni in Saudi Arabia and Shia in Iran will sit down again, as they once did before the Iranian Revolution."

She talked about enhancing the Iranian nuclear deal and dealing with the Taliban in giving them say in the new Afghani government. With the new transaction, the United States would shut down all military bases in Afghanistan, Iraq, and Syria, with France and Israel doing the same.

It was a bold speech, especially after surviving an assassination attempt and still not knowing who had done it, Bailey thought. *Could have been the Saudis. Then this whole speech might be a waste of time*, Bailey thought. She had pissed off the minister of petroleum and natural resources. However, he knew it was probably not the Saudis or any simple fanatical group. He had a strong hunch the ANU and Arthur Duran, a.k.a. John Birch, were somehow the culprit.

INTERVIEW WITH AN ELEVEN-YEAR-OLD REPORTER

On World Peace

We have a long way to go because of so many ideas and so much diversity, mental illness, and shortsightedness. An example of peace is talking to Cuba after sixty years of discomfort. We have now normalized relations, reopened the US embassy in Havana, and lifted travel restrictions and some sanctions. Some people don't want to see this happen. I say to them, how can you make peace with the world if you can't make peace with your neighbor?

—Sarah Hughes

CHAPTER 14

London, England, Friday One Month Later

12:00 p.m.

Bailey observed Hughes staring out the huge windows in the state dining room of the Lancaster House. He often wondered what her thoughts were regarding many quagmires around the globe. The first problem was her own attempted assassination.

The Islamic State of Iraq and the Levant had claimed responsibility for the assault on the president, and that was what the media reported. Indeed, all six gunmen were part of the Islamic State, with four more coconspirators discovered by the Mabahith.

Two terrorists had died at the scene, and another had died in the hospital. Three had been captured in the act, including one who left with a broken arm courtesy of the president. All four of Bailey's SADP had been hospitalized for gunshot wounds and recovered, except one was paralyzed. One bystander also had recovered from a gunshot wound, and Hughes had personally visited the individual. Hughes's Gallup poll approval rating, after that month and speech, went from 60 percent to 70. Most Americans rallied around Hughes's idea of the US military leaving the Middle East.

After the SADP conducted their own interrogations of the conspirators, they traced funds given to them by Brett McMahon, the bodyguard of Ian Blair. In learning more about Brett McMahon, they found he'd had a surgical facelift and now went by the name Simon Ellis and was a mercenary commanding a paramilitary. *We now don't know what he looks like*, Bailey thought, *or who he is working for, except the correlation to Blair.* The overlap in the people associated with President Adeyemi's death and with Hughes's attempted assassination was uncanny.

At the fifty-fifth G7 summit, Hughes winked at Bailey and moved past Ian Blair as everyone moved toward a large, well-dressed table in the center of the hall for tea break. Biscuits, tea, fruits, and sandwiches perfectly decorated the table as the prime ministers of Canada, Germany, Italy, Japan, and the United Kingdom and the president of France gathered around. Invited guests, presidents, and prime ministers of India, Australia, Chile, Egypt, and Nigeria also occupied the banquet hall, eating amid casual chatter. They had gathered to confer on the issues of unfair global trade, modernization of international taxation, objectives on the Iran nuclear deal, support of the African Union, stability in Libya, and the Russian military intervention in Ukraine.

Earlier, Bailey had watched Hughes speak to the new president of Nigeria, Shehu Jonathan, who privately had thanked her for the information on the mercenary Simon Ellis as it related to Adeyemi's assassination. Ellis was now being hunted in Nigeria, and the HMM project had started up again. Then there was Ian Blair, who Bailey had thought was just the CEO of Hoffro Holdings. He now knew Blair was an economist, one of the heads of several international organizations, and acting managing director of the International Monetary Fund, which was why he was there at the summit. Bailey sensed something sinister about the dude. He had no reason to prejudge Blair, but it was his gut feeling, and he believed POTUS felt the same.

Ever since the recent assassination attempt, Hughes had kept Bailey closer. She would show curiosity in trying to court with him. He would cheerfully decline and say, "How would it seem, Madam President, for a Secret Service agent to date you?"

"My favorite gorilla," she would say sarcastically, rolling her eyes in wonder. He thought it peculiar and too controversial to date the most powerful woman in the world.

Bailey focused on the moment and the exchange he heard between the president and Blair. Hughes already had been briefed on Blair, who he was, and his associates. Being the scrupulous person she was, she had analyzed Blair more, Bailey knew. They knew Blair was directly connected to the mercenary Ellis but couldn't yet prove it. They knew he was somehow connected to the ANU and John Birch, a.k.a. Arthur Duran, but couldn't prove it. Bailey knew that infuriated her. She was many things, including calculating and inquisitive.

When Hughes and Blair passed each other, Blair smiled, but Hughes did not.

With a frown, she spoke to him. "The soul has no secret that the behavior does not reveal."

He looked at her oddly as she continued past him toward the table.

Later in the day, before having another private meeting with the participating leaders, Hughes gave Bailey a task. "Give Agent Foreshadow the case," she told him, not looking him in the face.

She moved about her profession with simplicity. It was a way she showed her superiority and her seriousness, he thought.

He wondered if her naive seed-of-healing message would be misplaced by hate. He was going to stick around and see these historic events come true. Bailey loved being apolitical, loved his country, loved jazz, and, most of all, loved Madam Hughes.

He grinned; she was truly the Little Lioness, a president of true grit.

TOP SECRET

ESM Project

Electromagnetic Spectrum Metamaterials

███████ device manufactured at ████████████████████ WPAFB. Theoretical physicist professor ███ ███ says ███ ███; █ ██. █ ███. Astrophysics ███████████████████████████████ plasma at certain density ███████. Formula ███████ ██ ███ reverse engineering. Research theories into ██████████ █████████████████████. EM ████████████████. ██████ █ multiple wavelengths. ████████████████████. ██████ active camouflage ████. ████████████████████. Have been successful in cloaking car, tank, F-117, FAXX, and SC-21.

Continued rumors of the following:

- UFO sightings over Ohio
- Foreign reverse engineering
- Lethal Autonomous weaponry

Please unredact ASAP.

—*Sarah Hughes*

CPSIA information can be obtained
at www.ICGtesting.com
Printed in the USA
BVHW032125160720
583853BV00001B/39

9 781728 365848